A B O O

V E R Y   SHORT   POEMS

This collection is for my mother.

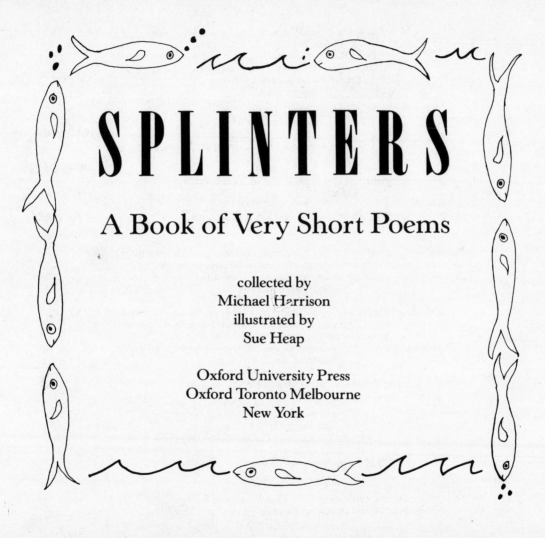

SPLINTERS

A Book of Very Short Poems

collected by
Michael Harrison
illustrated by
Sue Heap

Oxford University Press
Oxford Toronto Melbourne
New York

Oxford University Press, Walton Street, Oxford OX2 6DP
Oxford New York Toronto
Delhi Bombay Calcutta Madras Karachi
Petaling Jaya Singapore Hong Kong Tokyo
Nairobi Dar es Salaam Cape Town
Melbourne Auckland

and associated companies in
Berlin Ibadan

Oxford is a trade mark of Oxford University Press

Selection, arrangement and additional matter
© Oxford University Press 1988
First published 1988
First published in the United States 1989

British Library Cataloguing in Publication Data

Splinters: a book of very short poems.
1. Children's poetry, English
I. Harrison, Michael.
821'.914'0809282   PR1195.C47

Library of Congress catalog card number: 88-12551

ISBN 0-19-276072-6

Typeset by Pentacor Ltd., High Wycombe, Bucks
Printed in Great Britain by Butler & Tanner Ltd., Frome

And The Days Are Not Full Enough

And the days are not full enough
And the nights are not full enough
And life slips by like a field mouse
    Not shaking the grass.

Ezra Pound

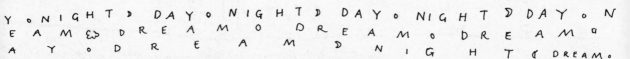

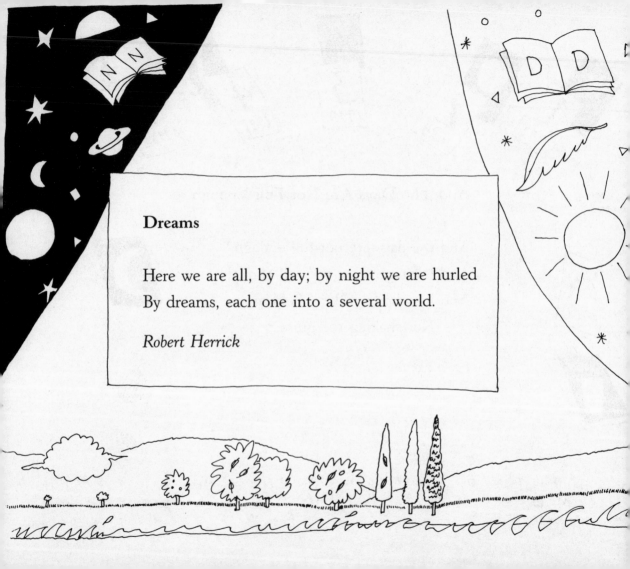

Dreams

Here we are all, by day; by night we are hurled
By dreams, each one into a several world.

Robert Herrick

The Warning

Just now,
Out of the strange
Still dusk . . . as strange as still . . .
A white moth flew.
Why am I grown so cold?

Adelaide Crapsey

Wind And Silver

Greatly shining,
The Autumn moon floats in the sky;
And the fish-ponds shake their backs and flash their
    dragon scales
As she passes over them.

Amy Lowell

A Clear Midnight

This is thy hour, O Soul, thy free flight into the
    wordless,
Away from books, away from art, the day erased, the
    lesson done,
Thee fully forth emerging, silent, gazing, pondering the
    themes thou lovest best,
Night, sleep, death and the stars.

Walt Whitman

Now Is A Ship

now is a ship

which captain am
sails out of sleep

steering for dream

e.e. cummings

Shadows

Chunks of night
Melt
In the morning sun.
One lonely one
Grows legs
And follows me
To school.

Patricia Hubbell

When I Was Three

When I was three I had a friend
Who asked me why bananas bend,
I told him why, but now I'm four,
I'm not so sure . . .

Richard Edwards

Halfway Street, Sidcup

'We did sums at school, Mummy—
you do them like this: look!' I showed her.

It turned out she knew already.

Fleur Adcock

Squeezes

We love to squeeze bananas,
We love to squeeze ripe plums,
And when they are feeling sad
We love to squeeze our mums.

Brian Patten

Mother Love

Mother love is a mighty benefaction
The prop of the world and its population
If mother love died the world would rue it
No money would bring the women to it.

Stevie Smith

A Sum

I give thee all, I can no more,
　　Though small thy share may be:
Two halves, three thirds, and quarters four
　　Is all I bring to thee.

Lewis Carroll

My Love For You

I know you little, I love you lots;
My love for you would fill ten pots,
Fifteen buckets, sixteen cans,
Three teacups and four dishpans.

Traditional

The Mermaid

Say not the mermaid is a myth,
I knew one once named Mrs Smith.
She stood while playing cards or knitting:
Mermaids are not equipped for sitting.

Ogden Nash

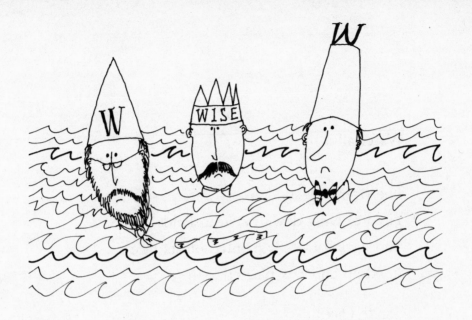

Three wise men of Gotham,
They went to sea in a bowl,
And if the bowl had been stronger
My song had been longer.

Anon

Waterfall

The river of a sudden
Tired of lying down between fields
And having the sky painted on its face
Stood up and was pleased.

Gareth Owen

To Old Age

I see in you the estuary that enlarges and spreads itself
grandly as it pours in the great sea.

Walt Whitman

The shy speechless sound
of a fruit falling from its tree,
and around it the silent music
of the forest, unbroken . . .

Osip Mandelstam

translated from the Russian by
Clarence Brown & W.S. Merwin

If I Walked Straight Slap

If I walked straight slap
Headlong down the road
Toward the two-wood gap
Should I hit that cloud?

Ivor Gurney

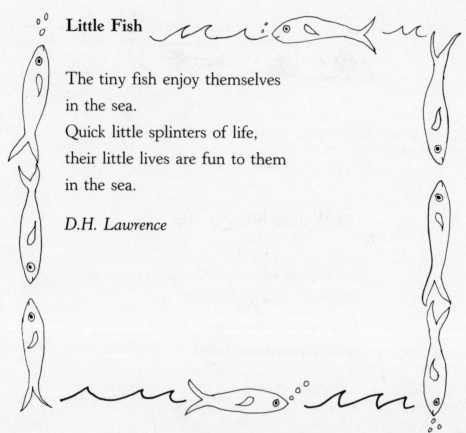

Little Fish

The tiny fish enjoy themselves
in the sea.
Quick little splinters of life,
their little lives are fun to them
in the sea.

D.H. Lawrence

Our Dog Chasing Swifts

A border collie has been bred to keep
Order among those wayward bleaters, sheep.
Ours, in a sheepless garden, vainly tries
To herd the screaming black sheep of the skies.

U.A. Fanthorpe

The Dog

The truth I do not stretch or shove
When I state the dog is full of love.
I've also proved, by actual test,
A wet dog is the lovingest.

Ogden Nash

Epitaph For A Good Mouser

Take, Lord, this soul of furred unblemished worth,
The sum of all I loved and caught on earth.
Quick was my holy purpose and my cause.
I die into the mercy of thy claws.

Anne Stevenson

Alley Cat

A bit of jungle in the street
He goes on velvet toes,
And slinking through the shadows, stalks
Imaginary foes.

Esther Valck Georges

The Greater Cats

The greater cats with golden eyes
Stare out between the bars.
Deserts are there, and different skies,
And night with different stars.

V. Sackville-West

Infant Innocence

The Grizzly Bear is huge and wild;
He has devoured the infant child.
The infant child is not aware
He has been eaten by the bear.

A.E. Housman

Season Song

Spring stirs slowly, shuffles, hops;
Summer dances close behind.
Autumn is a jostling crowd
but Winter creeps into your mind.

Judith Nicholls

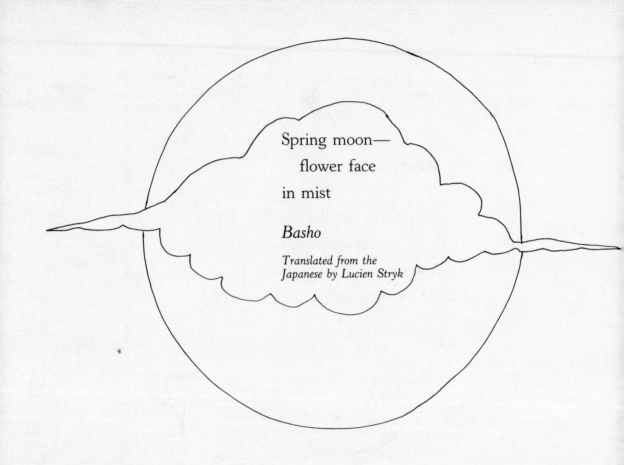

Spring moon—

flower face

in mist

Basho

Translated from the
Japanese by Lucien Stryk

April Gale

The wind frightens my dog, but I bathe in it,
Sound, rush, scent of the spring fields.

My dog's hairs are blown like feathers askew,
My coat's a demon, torturing like life.

Ivor Gurney

March

A blue day,
a blue jay
and a good beginning.
One crow, melting snow—
spring's winning!

Elizabeth Coatsworth

Spring

Spring
slips
silent
snowdrops
past Winter's iron gate.

Then daffodils'
golden trumpets
sound:
Victory!

Hugo Majer

The Locust Tree In Flower

Among
of
green

stiff
old
bright

broken
branch
come

white
sweet
May

again.

William Carlos Williams

Lesson From A Sundial

Ignore dull days; forget the showers;
Keep count of only shining hours.

Found on a sundial in Germany

Nature Poem

Skylark, what prompts your silver song
To fountain up and down the sky?

Beetles roast
With fleas on toast
And earthworm pie.

Adrian Mitchell

The Man In The Wilderness

The man in the wilderness asked of me,
How many strawberries grew in the sea?
I answered him as I thought good
As many red herrings as grew in a wood.

Anon

Radish

The radish is
the only dish
that isn't flat
but spherical.

Eating small
green peas off it
could make you quite
hysterical.

N.M. Bodecker

38

Tomato Ketchup

If you do not shake the bottle
None'll come and then a lot'll.

Anon

Hailstorm In May

Strike, churl; hurl, cheerless wind, then; heltering hail
May's beauty massacre and wispèd wild clouds grow
Out on the giant air; tell Summer No,
Bid joy back, have at the harvest, keep Hope pale.

Gerard Manley Hopkins

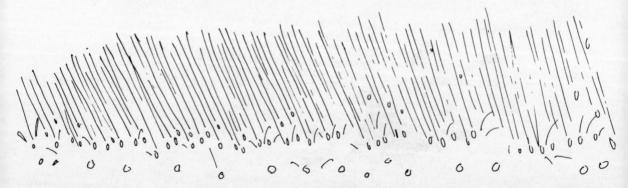

The Cherry Trees

The cherry trees bend over and are shedding
On the old road where all that passed are dead,
Their petals, strewing the grass as for a wedding
This early May morn when there is none to wed.

Edward Thomas

Bee

You want to make some honey?
All right. Here's the recipe.
Pour the juice of a thousand flowers
Through the sweet tooth of a Bee.

X.J. Kennedy

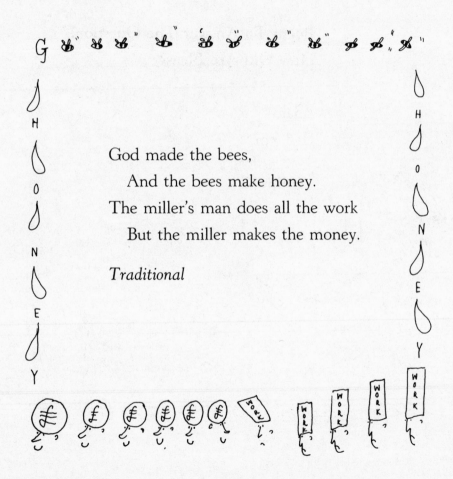

God made the bees,
And the bees make honey.
The miller's man does all the work
But the miller makes the money.

Traditional

Poem To Answer The Question:
How Old Are Fleas?

Adam
Had 'em

Traditional

The Tickle Rhyme

'Who's that tickling my back?' said the wall.
'Me,' said a small
Caterpillar. 'I'm learning
To crawl.'

Ian Serraillier

Caterpillar's Lullaby

Your sleep will be
a lifetime
and all your dreams
rainbows.
Close your eyes
and spin yourself
a fairytale:
Sleeping Ugly,
Waking Beauty.

Jane Yolen

The Early Morning

The moon on the one hand, the dawn on the other:
The moon is my sister, the dawn is my brother.
The moon on my left hand and the dawn on my right.
My brother, good morning: my sister, good night.

Hilaire Belloc

Written In An Album

Small service is true service while it lasts;
Of friends, however humble, scorn not one;
The daisy, by the shadow that it casts,
Protects the lingering dewdrop from the sun.

William Wordsworth

Where Innocent Bright-Eyed Daisies Are

Where innocent bright-eyed daisies are,
With blades of grass between,
Each daisy stands up like a star
Out of a sky of green.

Christina Rossetti

The Nest

Four blue stones in this thrush's nest
I leave, content to make the best
Of turquoise, lapis lazuli
Or for that matter of the whole blue sky.

Andrew Young

Bird Sips Water

Bird
sips water
drips music
throwing back its head

throw back your head
turn the rain
into a song
and you will fly

Keith Bosley

Love Without Hope

Love without hope, as when the young bird-catcher
Swept off his tall hat to the squire's own daughter,
So let the imprisoned larks escape and fly
Singing about her head, as she rode by.

Robert Graves

The Blue Room

My room is blue, the carpet's blue,
The chairs are blue, the door's blue too.
A blue bird flew in yesterday,
I don't know if it's flown away.

Richard Edwards

The White Thought

I shall be glad to be silent, Mother, and hear you speak,
You encouraged me to tell too much, and my thoughts are weak,
I shall keep them to myself for a time, and when I am older
They will shine as a white worm shines under a green boulder.

Stevie Smith

Clockface

Hours pass
slowly as a snail
creeping between the grassblades
of the minutes.

Judith Thurman

IX   X   XI   XII

Dandelions

Such brazen slatterns:
but later, whitehaired, genteel.

Gerda Mayer

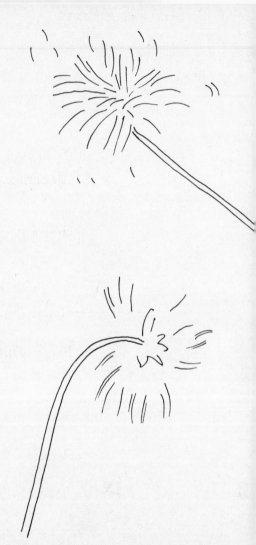

In Memoriam
(Easter, 1915)

The flowers left thick at nightfall in the wood
This Eastertide call into mind the men
Now far from home, who, with their sweethearts should
Have gathered them and will never do again.

Edward Thomas

Summer grasses,
all that remains
of soldiers' dreams.

Basho

Translated from the
Japanese by Lucien Stryk

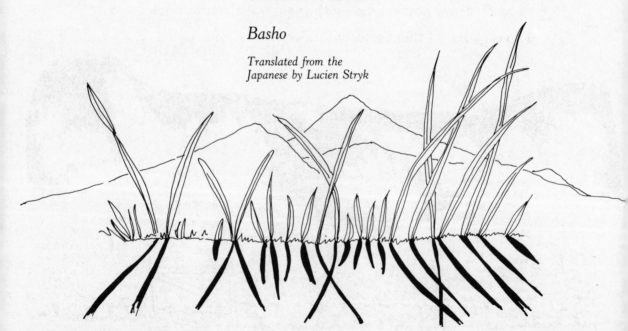

Napoleon

'What is the world, O Soldiers?
　　It is I:
I, this incessant snow,
　　This northern sky;
Soldiers, this solitude
　　Through which we go
　　Is I.'

Walter de la Mare

Here Dead Lie We

Here dead lie we because we did not choose
To live and shame the land from which we sprung.
Life, to be sure, is nothing much to lose;
But young men think it is, and we were young.

A.E. Housman

Harlech Castle

Here, decayed, an old
Giant's molar. It ground men's
Bones; their blood its bread.

John Corben

The Butterfly

A book of summer is the butterfly:
The print is small and hard to read,
The pages ruffle in the wind,
And when you close them up they die.

John Fuller

On The Beach

The waves claw
At the shingle
Time after time.
They fall back
Again and again,
Sighing, sighing.

John Corben

Fly Away, Fly Away

Fly away, fly away over the sea,
Sun-loving swallow, for summer is done;
Come again, come again, come back to me,
Bringing the summer and bringing the sun.

Christina Rossetti

Bilberries

on the hillside
in shaggy coats
hobgoblin fruit
easy for little
hands

Gerda Mayer

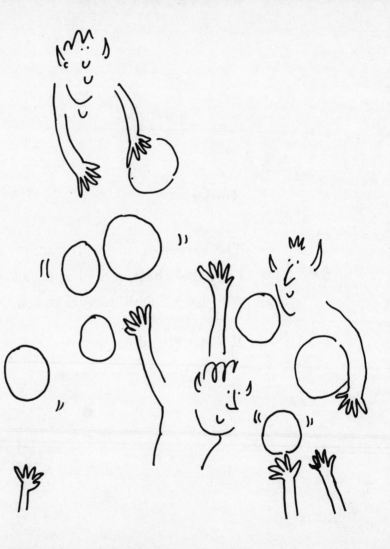

Rustler

The harvest-mouse with caution walks—
Only the wheat in a whisper talks—
All ears . . . with eyes on stalks.

William Stroud

The Fairy Ring

Here the horse-mushrooms make a fairy ring,
  Some standing upright and some overthrown,
A small Stonehenge, where heavy black slugs cling
  And bite away, like Time, the tender stone.

Andrew Young

Fog

The fog comes
on little cat feet.

It sits looking
over harbor and city
on silent haunches
and then moves on.

Carl Sandburg

The Sun and Fog contested
The Government of Day—
The Sun took down his yellow whip
And drove the Fog away.

Emily Dickinson

Splinter

The voice of the last cricket
across the first frost
is one kind of good-bye.
It is so thin a splinter of singing.

Carl Sandburg

Poor Adam and Eve were from Eden turned out
As a punishment due to their sin.
But here after eight, if you loiter about
As a punishment you'll be locked in.

On a Seat in Kensington Gardens (1844)

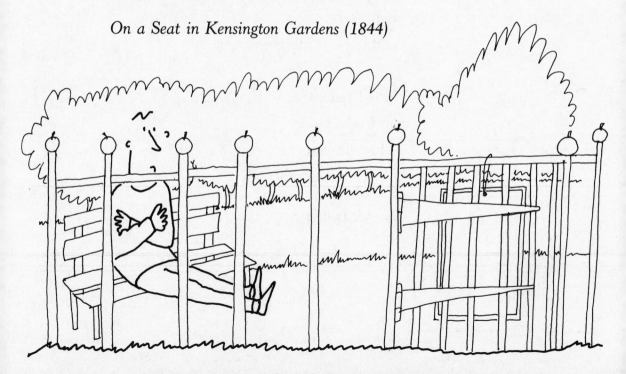

Small Rains

Bedtime tears
and evening sorrow,
here today
and gone tomorrow.

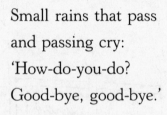

Small rains that pass
and passing cry:
'How-do-you-do?
Good-bye, good-bye.'

N. M. Bodecker

Prayer

Grant that no Hobgoblins fright me,
No hungry devils rise up and bite me;
No Urchins, Elves or drunkard Ghosts
Shove me against walls or posts.

John Day

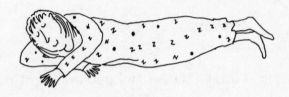

Good Night

Here's a body – there's a bed!
There's a pillow – here's a head!
There's a curtain – here's a light!
There's a puff – and so good night!

Thomas Hood

PUFF

GOODNIGHT

A Baby-Sermon

The lightning and thunder
　　They go and they come;
But the stars and the stillness
　　Are always at home.

George Macdonald

Others

'Mother, oh mother! where shall we hide us?
Others there are in the house beside us –
Moths and mice and crooked brown spiders!'

James Reeves

November Night

Listen . . .
With faint dry sound,
Like steps of passing ghosts,
The leaves, frost-crisped, break from the trees
And fall.

Adelaide Crapsey

The Christmas Spider

My fine web sparkles:
Indoor star in the roof's night
Over the baby.

Michael Richards

The Redbreast

The redbreast smoulders in the waste of snow:
His eye is large and bright, and to and fro
He draws and draws his slender threads of sound
Between the dark boughs and the freezing ground.

Anthony Rye

Gales

Weather buffets our houses in armour all night.
There is no sleep that is not a war with sound.
Morning is safer. A good view of the battleground.
And no roof that is not between light and light.

Anne Stevenson

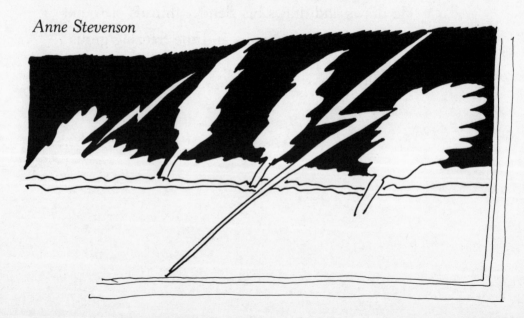

From the winter wind
a cold fly
came to our window
where we had frozen our noses
and warmed his feet on the glass

Michael Rosen

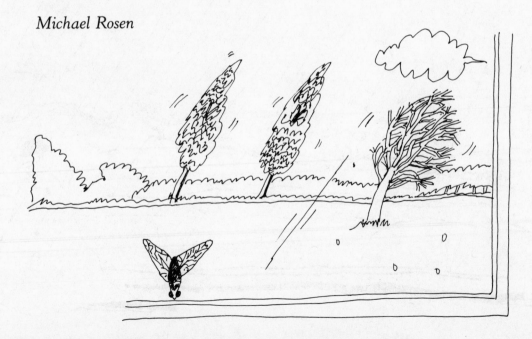

Snowman in a field
listening to the raindrops
wishing him farewell.

Roger McGough

Winter Wise

Walk fast in snow, in frost walk slow,
And still as you go tread on your toe;
When frost and snow are both together,
Sit by the fire, and spare shoe leather.

Traditional

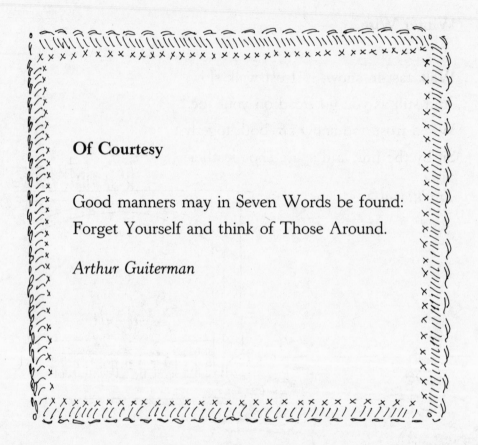

Of Courtesy

Good manners may in Seven Words be found:
Forget Yourself and think of Those Around.

Arthur Guiterman

The Parent

Children aren't happy with nothing to ignore,
And that's what parents were created for.

Ogden Nash

Eternity

He who binds to himself a joy
Does the winged life destroy;
But he who kisses the joy as it flies
Lives in eternity's sun rise.

William Blake

Things Made By Iron

Things made by iron and handled by steel are born
 dead,
   they are shrouds, they soak life out of us.
Till after a long time, when they are old and have steeped
   in our life
They begin to be soothed and soothing: then we throw them
  away.

D. H. Lawrence

Snow Poem

Winter
morning.
Snowflakes
for breakfast.
The street
outside
quiet
as a
long
white
bandage.

Roger McGough

On my winter walk
I see a riddle. Look there!
Water turned to bone.

Hugo Majer

from an Anglo-Saxon Riddle

Conceit

I heard a winter tree in song.
Its leaves were birds, a hundred strong;
When all at once it ceased to sing
For every leaf had taken wing.

Mervyn Peake

Thaw

Over the land freckled with snow half-thawed
The speculating rooks at their nests cawed
And saw from elm-tops, delicate as flower of grass,
What we below could not see, Winter pass.

Edward Thomas

I saw Esau sawing wood,
And Esau saw I saw him;
Though Esau saw I saw him saw,
Still Esau went on sawing.

Anon

Jack

That's Jack;
Lay a stick on his back!
What's he done? I cannot say.
We'll find out tomorrow,
And beat him today.

Charles Henry Ross

Don't care was made to care,
Don't care was hung;
Don't care was put in the pot
And boiled till he was done.

Traditional

529 1983

Absentmindedly,
sometimes,
I lift the receiver
And dial my own number.

(What revelations,
I think then,
If only
I could get through to myself.)

Gerda Mayer

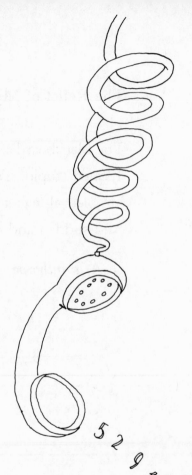

The Relief of Myopia

The blackboard's white turned dark; I
Turned stupid. Teachers noticed. The optician's
Jumbled alphabet foxed me. A load for my nose.
And sudden and beautiful eyebrows flared on faces.

U. A. Fanthorpe

What Are Heavy?

What are heavy? Sea-sand and sorrow;
What are brief? Today and Tomorrow;
What are frail? Spring blossoms and youth;
What are deep? The ocean and truth.

Christina Rossetti

Diary

Got up, went to school,
did homework, went to bed.

All that is net: life's
quick fish escaped.

M. J. Wilson

They might not need me – yet they might –
I'll let my heart be just in sight –
A smile so small as mine might be
Precisely their necessity.

Emily Dickinson

Fragment

as for him who
finds fault
may silliness

and sorrow
overtake him
when you wrote

you did not
know
the power of

your words.

William Carlos Williams

Beyond Words

That row of icicles along the gutter
Feels like my armoury of hate;
And you, you . . . you, you utter . . .
You wait.

Robert Frost

Choose

The single clenched fist lifted and ready,
Or the open asking hand held out and waiting.
Choose:
For we meet by one or the other.

Carl Sandburg

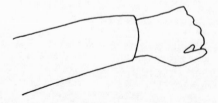
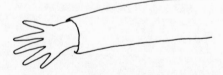

Happy Thought

The world is so full of a number of things,
I'm sure we should all be as happy as kings.

Robert Louis Stevenson

Ease

Lined coat, warm cap and easy felt slippers,
In the little tower, at the low window, sitting over the
  sunken brazier.
Body at rest, heart at peace; no need to rise early.
I wonder if the courtiers at the Western Capital know of
  these things, or not?

Po Chu-I

(835 A.D.)
Translated from the Chinese by Arthur Waley

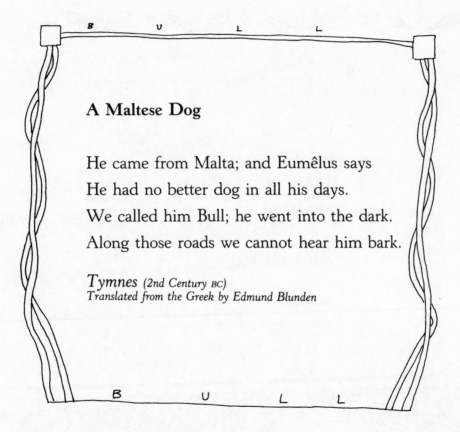

A Maltese Dog

He came from Malta; and Eumêlus says
He had no better dog in all his days.
We called him Bull; he went into the dark.
Along those roads we cannot hear him bark.

Tymnes (2nd Century BC)
Translated from the Greek by Edmund Blunden

In the eggs
the chickens say,
'Don't count
your foxes
before
you're hatched.'

John Corben

No lake is so still but that it has its wave;

No circle so perfect but that it has its blur.

I would change things for you if I could;

As I can't, you must take them as they are.

Old Chinese Rhyming Proverb

Translated by Arthur Waley

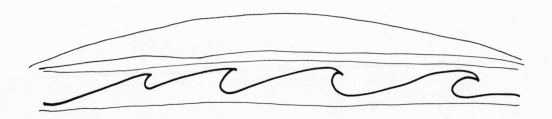

WIND

RRAIN
NRAIN
RRAIN

Z
Z
Z
Z
Z
Z
Z
Z
Z
Z
Z

Good Appetite

Of breakfast, then of walking to the pond;
Of wind, work, rain, and sleep I never tire.
God of monotony, may you be fond
Of me and these forever, and wood fire.

Mark Van Doren

WOOD

The Four Best Things

Health is the first good lent to men;
A gentle disposition then:
Next, to be rich by no by-ways;
Lastly, with friends t'enjoy our days.

Translated from the Greek by Robert Herrick

Be Like The Bird

Be like the bird, who
Resting in his flight
On a twig too slight
Feels it bend beneath him,
Yet sings
Knowing he has wings.

Victor Hugo

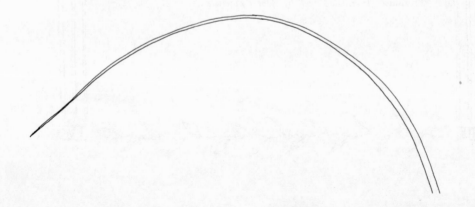

The Tin Frog

I have hopped, when properly wound up, the whole length
Of the hallway; once hopped halfway down the stairs,
   and fell.
Since then the two halves of my tin have been awry; my
   strength
Is not quite what it used to be; I do not hop so well.

Russell Hoban

I give you the end of a golden string;
 Only wind it into a ball,
It will lead you in at Heaven's gate,
 Built in Jerusalem's wall.

William Blake

From Prison

You took away all the oceans and all the room.
You gave me my shoe-size in earth with bars around it.
Where did it get you? Nowhere.
You left me my lips, and they shape words, even in
  silence.

Osip Mandelstam

Quatrain: Poet

To clothe the fiery thought
In simple words succeeds,
For still the craft of genius is
To mask a king in weeds.

Ralph Waldo Emerson

The Coming Of Good Luck

So good luck came, and on my roof did light
Like noiseless snow, or as the dew of night:
Not all at once, but gently, as the trees
Are by the sunbeams tickled by degrees.

Robert Herrick

Index Of Titles And First Lines (Where Untitled)

Acknowledgements

The editor and publisher are grateful for permission to include the following copyright poems in this anthology:

Fleur Adcock: "Halfway Street Sidcup" from *The Incident Book*, © Fleur Adcock 1986. Reprinted by permission of Oxford University Press.   **Basho**, trs. Lucien Stryk: "Spring moon" and "Summer Grasses" from *On Love and Barley*. Reprinted by permission of the translator.   **Hilaire Belloc**: "The Early Morning" from *Collected Poems*. Reprinted by permission of Gerald Duckworth & Co. Ltd.   **Edmund Blunden**, trans.: "A Maltese Dog", translated from the Greek of Tymnes and reprinted from *From the Greek* (Clarendon Press) by permission of A.D. Peters & Co. Ltd.   **N.M. Bodecker**: "Radish" and "Small Rains" from *Snowman Sniffles*. Copyright © 1983 N.M. Bodecker. Reprinted by permission of Atheneum Publishers, a division of Macmillan, Inc., and Faber & Faber Ltd.   **Keith Bosley**: "Bird" from *And I Dance*. Copyright © Keith Bosley 1972. Reprinted by permission of Angus & Robertson (UK) Ltd.   **Elizabeth Coatsworth**: "March". Reprinted with permission of Macmillan Publishing Company from *Summer Green* by Elizabeth Coatsworth. Copyright 1948 by Macmillan Publishing Company, renewed 1976 by Elizabeth Coatsworth Beston.   **John Corben**: "Harlech Castle", "On the Beach" and "In the Eggs . . .". Reprinted with permission.   **e.e. Cummings**: "now is a ship", copyright © 1960 by e.e. cummings. Reprinted from *Complete Poems 1913–1962* by permission of Grafton Books, A Division of the Collins Publishing Group, and Harcourt Brace Jovanovich Inc.   **Walter de la Mare**: "Napoleon". Reprinted by permission of The Literary Trustees of Walter de la Mare and The Society of Authors as their representative.   **Emily Dickinson**: "The Sun and Fog contested . . ." and "They might not need me-yet they might- . . .". Reprinted by permission of the publishers and the Trustees of Amherst College from *The Poems of Emily Dickinson*, edited by Thomas H. Johnson, Cambridge, Mass.: The Belknap Press of Harvard University, Copyright 1951, © 1951, © 1955, 1979, 1983 by The President and Fellows of Harvard College.   **Richard Edwards**: "When I Was Three" and "The Blue Room", © Richard Edwards, from *The Word Party*, Lutterworth Press 1986. Used by permission of John Johnson (Authors' Agent) Ltd. and the publisher.   **U.A. Fanthorpe**: "Our dog chasing Swifts" and "The Relief of Myopia", both © 1988 U.A. Fanthorpe. Reprinted by permission of the author.   **Robert Frost**: "Beyond Words" from *The Poetry of Robert Frost*, ed. Edward Connery Lathem. Copyright © 1969 by Holt, Rinehart and

118

119

A BOOK OF

VERY SHORT POEMS